THE GEEZER IN THE FREEZER

Randall Wright

ILLUSTRATED BY Thor Wickstrom

BLOOMSBURY

NEW YORK BERLIN LONDON

Published by Bloomsbury U.S.A. Children's Books
175 Fifth Avenue, New York, New York 10010

Library of Congress Cataloging-in-Publication Data
Wright, Randall.
The geezer in the freezer / by Randall Wright ;
illustrated by Thor Wickstrom.—1st U.S. ed.
        p.   cm.
Summary: Stuck between a rump roast and a pie, the old man
living in the freezer finally gets to tell his tale of woe.
ISBN-13: 978-1-59990-135-0 · ISBN-10: 1-59990-135-8 (hardcover)
ISBN-13: 978-1-59990-390-3 · ISBN-10: 1-59990-390-3 (reinforced)
[1. Stories in rhyme. 2. Humorous stories.] I. Wickstrom, Thor, illus. II. Title.
PZ8.3.W9368Ge 2009   [Fic]—dc22   2009004631

Art created with oil paint on prepared paper
Typeset in Hank
Book design by Donna Mark

First U.S. Edition 2009
Printed in China by SNP Leefung Printers Limited
2 4 6 8 10 9 7 5 3 1 (hardcover)
2 4 6 8 10 9 7 5 3 1 (reinforced)

For three cool dudes: Evan, Parker, and Ethan
—R. W.

For my dear old mother and her geezer, Harold
—T. W.

There's a geezer in our freezer
and he's shiverin' fit to die,
with his feet upon a rump roast
and his elbow in a pie!

Maybe someone put him in there
just to keep him for a while,
but it gives me crawly creepies
'cause he's frozen with a smile.

I was huntin' for some ice cream
and I knew we had a stash
right betwixt the Christmas turkey
and the frozen corned-beef hash.

As I rummaged in that icebox
I was taken with a chill,
'cause I sensed two eyes upon me
and I felt an eerie thrill.

Then I spied him in the corner
huddled back amongst the peas,
and I started in to holler—
but he stopped me with a sneeze.

"It's so cold in here," he chattered,
"could you let me have a coat?
Or somethin' warm and woolly
I kin wrap around my throat?"

Well, I shut that door right smartly.
Wouldn't you have done it too,
if a coot was in your freezer
with his edges turnin' blue?

When I told Aunt May about him,
she replied, "WHY, THAT'S ABSURD!"
(She's a little hard of hearing,
so she shouted every word.)

"DON'T YOU THINK THAT I'DA NOTICED
SOMETHIN' LIKE A CHATTERIN' GENT?"
(Well, I guess she maybe would've,
'cept her eyesight's nearly spent.)

Wasn't long again I saw him
(Aunt May sent me for some corn).
He was shiverin' by the ham bone,
and his face looked so forlorn.

"Kin you spare a bite of somethin'
for to warm me up a touch?
I'm so tired of eatin' snow crab.
Maybe chili beans or such?"

When I spoke of it to Auntie,
she just squinted up her eyes
(like I said, her vision's failin'
though she's hardy otherwise).

"WELL, I THINK THAT FREEZER'S HAUNTED
BY THE GHOSTS OF SUPPERS PAST,
'CAUSE I SOMETIMES HEAR FAINT WHISPERS . . ."

I was sorry now I asked.

'Twas a Friday night I reckon
that I met him once again.
I was off to fetch some taters
from the garden produce bin.

Sure as shootin' he was in there,
icy-haired just like before,
with a frost upon his eyebrows—
well, I had to shut that door!

"Now you wait a goldarn minute,"
cried that geezer with a squeak.
"I don't think that I kin take it—
not another blasted week."

I kinda froze a minute—
almost two—and then I spoke.
"Whatchoo doin' in our icebox?
Where you from, and where's your folk?"

Well, his eyes turned far and misty
and a tear ran down his nose,
where it made a little rainbow
in the light, and then *it* froze.

"'Tis a tale that's long in tellin'," said that geezer with a sigh, "but I reckon I should tell it once or twice before I die.

"I was sent to fetch some vittles
by the woman I adore,
and I paused in here to ponder
on the joys of sweet *amour*.

"But I tarried much too long here
and I fear her love's grown old,
and I reckon she's forgot me
or she thinks my heart's turned cold.

"See, I met her in the springtime
when the blush was on the rose,
and we courted through the summer,
sippin' sodas nose to nose.

"In the fall we thought we'd marry
at the church away in town,
then we'd snuggle up together
while the winter hunkered down.

"But we never saw the snowfall,
nor in autumn did we wed.
I've been stuck here in this freezer!"
were the words the old man said.

"I cain't budge one way or t'other,
I cain't even turn about.
Guess I'm froze in here forever—
'spect I'm never comin' out."

I was quiet for a second,
but I couldn't hold it in.
That old laughin' burbled upward—
first it started with a grin.

Then it burst right out with hiccups
and I rolled upon the floor,
and I giggled and I snorted
till I couldn't laugh no more.

"Looky here, you silly geezer,
at that switch there on your right.
It's a self-defrostin' freezer—
it'll do it overnight."

Then I pushed that button for him, and I went upstairs to sleep.

When I came back in the mornin' there was water two feet deep.

And that frozen pop was sittin'
on the stove with eyes aglow,
while my aunt May stood there squintin'
at her thawed-out Romeo.

"IS THAT YOU, MY FROSTBIT PUMPKIN?
HOW I'VE MISSED MY DARLING MAN."
That old gent just sorta giggled,
then he blushed and kissed her hand.

Now that codger is our lodger,
and he's livin' right downstairs
in the room next to the furnace—
says he's done with Frigidaires.